DATE DUE

JUN 0 4 2014			

RECEIVED

DEC 0 5 2012

GREENWOOD PUBLIC LIBRARY

DISCARDED

WEATHER and CLIMATE

Extreme Weather

Robin Birch

MACMILLAN LIBRARY

First published in 2009 by
MACMILLAN EDUCATION AUSTRALIA PTY LTD
15–19 Claremont Street, South Yarra 3141

Visit our website at www.macmillan.com.au or go directly to www.macmillanlibrary.com.au
Associated companies and representatives throughout the world.

Copyright © Robin Birch 2009

All rights reserved.
Except under the conditions described in the *Copyright Act 1968* of Australia
and subsequent amendments, no part of this publication may be reproduced,
stored in a retrieval system, or transmitted in any form or by any means,
electronic, mechanical, photocopying, recording or otherwise, without the
prior written permission of the copyright owner.

Educational institutions copying any part of this book for educational purposes
under the Act must be covered by a Copyright Agency Limited (CAL) licence
for educational institutions and must have given a remuneration notice to CAL.
Licence restrictions must be adhered to. Any copies must be photocopies only,
and they must not be hired out or sold. For details of the CAL licence contact:
Copyright Agency Limited, Level 15, 233 Castlereagh Street, Sydney, NSW 2000.
Telephone: (02) 9394 7600. Facsimile: (02) 9394 7601. Email: info@copyright.com.au

National Library of Australia Cataloguing-in-Publication data

Birch, Robin.
    Extreme weather / Robin Birch.

    9781420265996 (hbk.)
    Weather and climate
    Includes index.
    For primary school age.
    Storms - Juvenile literature.
        Weather - Juvenile literature
551.55

Edited by Kylie Cockle
Text and cover design by Marta White
Page layout by Marta White
Photo research by Legend Images
Illustrations by Gaston Vanzet

Printed in China

Acknowledgements
The author and the publisher are grateful to the following for permission to reproduce copyright material:
Front cover photograph: Lightning © Marinko Tarlac/Shutterstock
Photos courtesy of:
AAP/AP Photo/Jamie Alexander, **20** (left); AAP/AP Photo/Pavel Rahman, **24**; AAP Image/Philip Quirk/Wildlight, **23** (top); © Commit/Dreamstime.com, **10** (top); © Duming/Dreamstime.com, **20** (right); © Kasiden/Dreamstime.com, **27**; © Kommaz/Dreamstime.com, **15**; © Petejw/Dreamstime.com, **29**; © Surpasspro/Dreamstime.com, **4**; Narinder Nanu/AFP/Getty Images, **22**; Jim Reed/Getty Images, **14**, **17** (bottom); © Mike Bentley/iStockphoto, **21** (right); © Chieh Cheng/iStockphoto, **17** (top); © Parker Deen/iStockphoto, **19**; © Gary Etchell/iStockphoto, **10** (bottom); © Alexander Hafemann/iStockphoto, **21** (left); © Mark Hayes/iStockphoto, **26** (top); © mcdc/iStockphoto, **6**; Gavin Mclaughlan, **28**; Jacques Descloitres, MODIS Land Rapid Response Team, NASA/GSFC, **16** (top); Data from NOAA GOES satellite. Image produced by Hal Pierce, Laboratory for Atmospheres, NASA Goddard Space Flight Center, **18**; National Science Foundation, photo by Josh Landis, **30**; Photolibrary/Yvette Cardozo, **5**; Photolibrary/OSF, **13** (left); Photolibrary/Jim Reed/SPL, **9**; Photolibrary/Jim Zuckerman, **13** (right); © Dainis Derics/Shutterstock, **26** (bottom); © Zastol`skiy Victor Leonidovich/Shutterstock, **12** (left); © viZualStudio/Shutterstock, **12** (right); USAID, photo by R. Nyberg, **23** (bottom); US Marines, photo by Lance Cpl. Raymond Petersen III, **25**; Wikimedia Commons, image created by Nilfanion. Background image from NASA Visible Earth. Tracking data for storms in the North Atlantic and East Pacific is from the National Hurricane Center. Tracking data for storms in the Indian Ocean, the Northwest Pacific and the South Pacific is from the Joint Typhoon Warning Center. Tracking data for Cyclone Catarina in the South Atlantic was produced by Roger Edson, University of Guam, **16** (bottom).

While every care has been taken to trace and acknowledge copyright, the publisher tenders their apologies for any accidental infringement where copyright has proved untraceable. Where the attempt has been unsuccessful, the publisher welcomes information that would redress the situation.

Contents

Weather and climate	4
Extreme weather	5
Thunderstorms	6
Tornadoes	12
Tropical storms	16
Extreme wind	20
Monsoon and drought	22
Floods and landslides	24
Ice and snow	26
Heatwaves and wildfires	28
Weather wonders	30
Glossary	31
Index	32

Glossary Words

When a word is printed in **bold**, you can look up its meaning in the Glossary on page 31.

Weather and climate

What is the weather like today? Is it hot, cold, wet, dry, windy or still? Is it frosty or snowy? Is there a storm on the way? We are all interested in the weather, because it makes a difference to how we feel, what we wear and what we can do.

The weather takes place in the air, and we notice it because air is all around us.

Climate

The word 'climate' describes the usual weather of a particular place. If a place usually has cold weather, then we say that place has a cold climate. If a place usually has hot weather, we say it has a hot climate.

Storms can cause serious damage to property.

Extreme weather

Sometimes weather is extreme. This means that the weather can be extremely hot, cold, windy, wet or dry. There can be violent storms, cold snaps, heatwaves, **droughts** or floods.

People need protection during times of extreme weather. Houses, buildings and crops can be destroyed. Many communities have systems in place to help and rescue people who are affected by extreme weather.

Some people live in places that have extreme weather climates all the time. Their shelter and clothing is designed to protect them from the weather. For example, the Inuit people who live in ice and snow wear warm furs and have warm houses. Many people who live in hot **deserts** wear clothing that protects them from the Sun.

This Inuit woman is ice fishing and is protected from the extreme weather by her clothing.

Thunderstorms

We know a thunderstorm is coming when we see dark clouds and lightning flashes in the sky. We might hear the crack of thunder and then expect rain, wind and perhaps hail.

Thunderstorms usually occur in warm, **humid** weather. They take place in all parts of the world except Antarctica.

Thunderclouds

Thunderclouds are called 'cumulonimbus' clouds. These clouds are very tall. They can reach right to the top of the **troposphere**, which may be up to 15 kilometres above Earth's surface. They look dark grey to us because they are so tall that very little sunlight can pass through them. The clouds often have wide, flat tops. The tops are flattened by cold winds that blow across them.

The cumulonimbus clouds show that a thunderstorm is approaching.

Inside a thundercloud

Thunderstorms occur when lots of warm, moist air rises. It rises because it has been pushed up by a **cold front**, or because warm sea below it has warmed it, or because bodies of unstable air meet each other.

When warm, moist air rises, it cools. As the air cools, **water vapour** in the air **condenses**, and makes water drops. At the top of the cloud, where it is very cold, tiny ice **crystals** form.

Winds rush upwards and downwards inside thunderclouds. This throws water and ice up and down. The movements of the air, water and ice create the electrical **charges** that cause lightning.

Weather Report

Winds that rush up and down inside thunderclouds are called 'updrafts' and 'downdrafts'. If an aircraft is caught flying in clouds with these winds, and is tossed around, we say the aircraft and its passengers are experiencing turbulence.

Warm air rises as a cold front approaches, making a cumulonimbus cloud. These clouds are full of water and ice.

cumulonimbus cloud

warm moist air rises

direction of cold front

Rain and hail

In thunderclouds, strong winds toss water and ice crystals up and down. Water freezes onto ice crystals, which can then form into ice balls called hailstones. These balls fall out of the clouds when they become too heavy, or they may be blown out in a strong downburst of wind.

Raindrops are formed from condensing air vapour and from hailstones that melt as they fall through warm air. They usually fall from thunderclouds in short, heavy showers. Sometimes the raindrops **evaporate** before they reach the ground. This can give a fringed appearance to the bottom of a thundercloud.

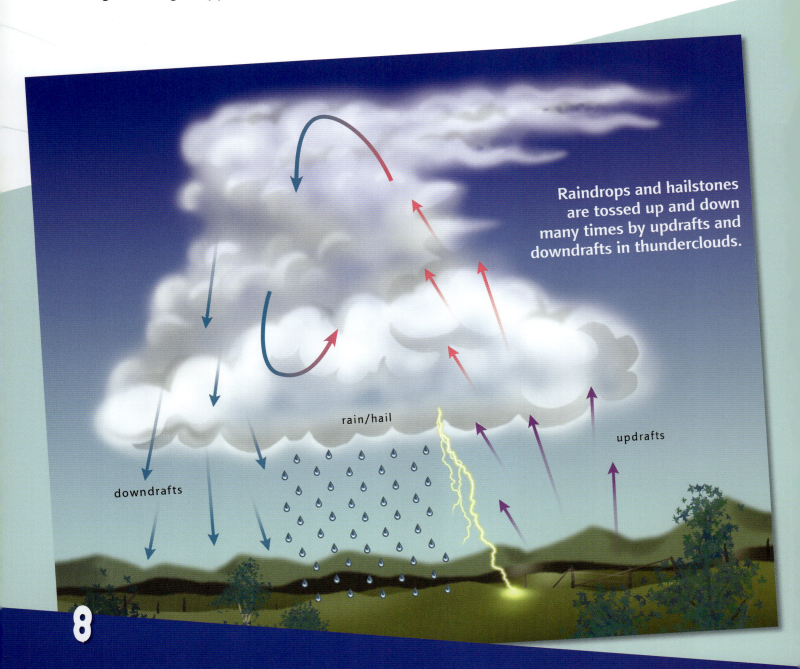

Raindrops and hailstones are tossed up and down many times by updrafts and downdrafts in thunderclouds.

Hailstones

Hailstones always come from thunderclouds. They are tossed up and down inside a thundercloud many times. At high, very cold levels, ice forms on them in a white layer. At lower, not-quite-so-cold levels, ice forms on them in a clear layer. By counting the white and clear layers in a hailstone we can see how many times it has been tossed up and down in a thundercloud.

Thunderstorms can take place in warm or cold weather. Ice balls that are made from rain that freezes when it meets cold air close to the ground are called 'ice pellets'. Ice pellets are only found in cold winter weather.

Weather Report

Hailstones that fall to the ground can be the size of a pea or bigger than a tennis ball. Large hailstones have caused enormous damage to crops.

Hailstorms can cause very unwelcome damage to cars and property.

Lightning and thunder

Lightning is a huge electrical spark produced by a thunderstorm. Lightning **bolts** are around 1.6 kilometres long, and they heat the nearby air to 10 000 degrees **Celsius**.

Thunder is the noise lightning makes. Lightning and thunder happen at the same time, but we see lightning before we hear it. This is because light travels faster than sound. Thunderstorms are known as an electrical storms.

Safety

The safest place to shelter during an electrical storm is in a building or a car. Do not stay outdoors. If there is no shelter, stay away from tall trees. It is possible to be struck by lightning in open areas.

Tall buildings often have special posts, called 'lightning rods', to send lightning safely down to the ground.

We see lightning before we hear it.

This tree was struck by lightning.

Types of lightning

There are a number of different types of lightning. The table below describes the four main types.

The four most common types of lightning

Type of lightning	Description
sheet	occurs inside thunderclouds most common form of lightning called sheet lightning, because large parts of clouds are lit up, which makes them look like a bright sheet
cloud-to-ground	second most common kind of lightning strikes trees, buildings, people and animals
cloud-to-cloud	lightning that can strike between thunderclouds
cloud-to-air	lightning that flashes from a cloud to the air around it

Unusual lightning

Ball lightning is an unusual kind of lightning. It is a glowing ball of lightning, usually 20 to 30 centimetres across. It can form in a room and fly out through a window.

Four different kinds of lightning

sheet

cloud-to-cloud

cloud-to-air

cloud-to-ground

Weather Report

Cloud-to-ground lightning can flash from the top of a thundercloud to the ground many kilometres away, where there is clear blue sky. This kind of lightning has given us the saying 'a bolt from the blue', which means something very unexpected has happened.

Tornadoes

Tornadoes, which are also called 'twisters', are funnels of rising wind that can suck up almost anything in their path. They often leave a terrible trail of destruction behind them – they can lift cars, uproot trees and tear houses and buildings apart. Tornadoes occur in many countries, but are most common in the mid-western part of the United States, in an area known as 'Tornado Alley'.

Tornadoes form during thunderstorms. We see them coming from the bottom of thunderclouds, and they often reach the ground.

Wind speeds of tornadoes

Tornado winds are the fastest, most violent winds known. Most tornadoes have wind speeds of up to 180 kilometres per hour, and are approximately 75 metres across.

Tornadoes move quickly across the ground and can change direction quickly and unexpectedly. Most travel for several kilometres and then disappear. Others stay on the ground for more than 100 kilometres.

Tornadoes form in thunderclouds.

Typical disaster damage caused by a tornado.

How tornadoes form

Tornadoes form from quickly rising air within a thundercloud. The rising air hits air that is moving in a different direction, and starts to rotate.

When the rising, rotating air keeps moving faster, the column of air grows larger and longer, and can reach to the ground. The rotating air moves so fast that it makes a loud noise.

Inside a tornado funnel, the air pressure is low. This causes cloud to form inside the funnel. The cloud is called 'funnel cloud', and it makes it easy to see tornadoes during the day. Tornado funnels pick up dust and dirt from the ground they cross, which also makes them easy to see.

At night, we can only see tornadoes if they are lit up by lightning in the storm cloud above.

The funnel cloud in this tornado is carrying a lot of dirt.

Tornado warnings

In areas where there are many tornadoes, weather officials keep a lookout for new tornadoes, and for thunderclouds that are likely to develop into tornadoes. They use **radar**, and trained volunteer tornado spotters keep watch.

If a tornado is spotted, or a thundercloud looks like it will develop into a tornado, a tornado warning is sent out, and **sirens** may be sounded. This is the time when people should move to their chosen safe place.

Tornado watchers

Some people enjoy watching tornadoes for interest, and so that they can warn others. They watch them so they can tell others what they have seen, and show them photos and movies that they have taken.

Storm watchers take risks to see whether thunderstorms will turn into tornadoes.

Strange events

Tornadoes can suck up almost everything in their path, and they are capable of carrying these things for long distances.

Tornadoes cause a huge amount of damage, and many people and animals have been killed by them. There have been some strange stories of survival, too. In 1995, a baby was pulled from his bed by a tornado and later found one kilometre away in a ditch. He was unhurt, apart from a few scratches.

Waterspouts are weak tornadoes. When a **waterspout** sucks up water, it also sucks up everything in the water. People have found fish, frogs, crabs and weeds falling from the sky many kilometres away from the water they came from.

Waterspouts form over water and suck it up.

Tropical storms

Tropical storms are the most extreme kinds of storms. They bring extreme wind, rain, waves, floods, lightning and thunder. Every year there are about 80 tropical storms in the world.

Tropical storms form in the tropics, which is the area around the middle of Earth, where it is hot and humid. They do not form at Earth's **equator**, but just on either side. They start out as thunderstorms over the ocean. Then they travel across the sea, away from the equator. Tropical storms gain strength as they go, but only if they are over warm water. They die away when they cross cool water or land.

Tropical storms are called 'hurricanes' in the United States, 'cyclones' around India and Australia, and 'typhoons' in parts of Asia.

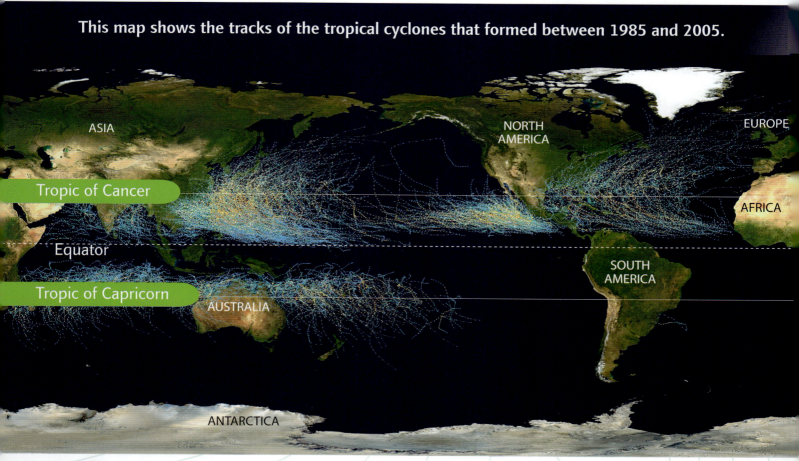

This map shows the tracks of the tropical cyclones that formed between 1985 and 2005.

How tropical storms form

In tropical areas, the sea is warm and the air is very humid. In very hot weather, the air rises quickly, and forms cumulonimbus clouds (thunderclouds). These clouds are very tall. They contain heavy rain, and produce thunder and lightning.

Winds rush from other areas to replace the rising air. The new air rises, too. By this time there is so much air quickly rising that the incoming winds start to spiral into the centre of the storm. They do not spiral if the thunderstorm is right over Earth's equator.

The upwards-rushing winds pull more and more moisture up from the sea and into the air, making bands of thundercloud. When the winds reach 118 kilometres per hour, the storm is called a hurricane, cyclone or typhoon.

A tropical storm strikes the coast.

Winds reach high speeds in tropical storms.

The eye of the storm

When a tropical storm hits land there are thunderstorms while one side of the storm passes over. The weather becomes calm as the centre goes over, then there are more thunderstorms as the other side passes.

The centre of a tropical storm is called the 'eye of the storm'. It has a huge rotating wall of thundercloud around it called the 'eyewall'. The eye is around 30 kilometres across, and the weather below it is calm, with no wind or rain. Air sinks in the eye, and the area will often have clear blue sky.

Storm surge

In tropical storms there is a lot of rising air. This sucks the surface of the ocean upwards, so that it rises. This uplifted water is called a 'storm surge', and it brings huge waves to the coast when the storm reaches land.

The eyewall of Hurricane Floyd, which struck the Bahamas and the east coast of the United States in September 1999

Damage and warnings

Tropical storms have caused billions of dollars worth of damage, and have killed many people.

Tropical storms travel across the sea at about 10 kilometres per hour. Weather authorities discover them in **satellite** photographs. Then they track them so they can warn ships at sea, and people on land if the storm is heading for land. The storms are usually given people's names, such as Cyclone Tracy or Hurricane Andrew.

The weather authorities send out storm warnings, mainly by radio, television and the Internet. If a storm approaches land, many people leave the area, and others try to find shelter in strong buildings.

The tropical storm Cyclone Nargis hit Burma and Sri Lanka in May 2008. The strong winds, heavy rains and floods damaged many thousands of buildings and it is estimated that one million people died.

Weather Report

In August 2005, Hurricane Katrina passed close to the city of New Orleans, in the United States. There was a huge storm surge, which broke the canal **levees** and flooded most of the city.

This terrible damage was caused by Hurricane Katrina.

Winds

Winds do not always have to be part of a thunderstorm to be extreme. Winds can whip up dust storms and sandstorms. They can also cause whirlwinds and strong sea winds.

Dust storms and sandstorms

When strong winds blow across dry land, dust storms and sandstorms occur. They take place in the world's hot deserts, and they also happen on land during a dry spell or drought. It is hard to see very far in a dust storm or sandstorm.

During dust storms, dust is whipped up into a huge cloud that may travel a long distance, so the dust moves from one place to another. This can strip farmland of its valuable soil, and leave other places covered in dust.

Memorable dust storms

The 1930s in the United States are known as 'the Dust Bowl years'. There was so much dust picked up by strong winds that it blew across the Atlantic Ocean to Europe.

In 1983 in south-east Australia, there was a huge dust storm that carried red dust over to New Zealand, and made **glaciers** turn red.

This huge dust cloud of topsoil rolled over Griffith in New South Wales, Australia in 2002.

Some places have such constant strong wind that it wears rock away.

Whirlwinds in desert areas often contain sand.

Whirlwinds

Whirlwinds are rotating funnels of air that are found in hot, dry places. They have many different names, such as 'dust devils', 'dancing devils' and 'willy-willies'. They are not formed from thunderclouds like tornadoes are. They do not usually cause any damage.

Sea winds

Strong winds at sea whip up huge waves, which can reach 20 metres or more in height. Sometimes these waves wash right over large ships. In 1995 in the North Atlantic Ocean, the ocean liner *The QEII* was hit by a 29-metre wave.

Weather Report

People in yacht races sometimes need to be rescued because the wind and waves are so extreme.

Lighthouses often have huge waves crash around them.

Monsoons and droughts

At different times and places on Earth, there can be monsoon conditions, when there is a lot of rain, and drought conditions, when there is a severe shortage of rainfall.

Monsoons

Monsoons are winds that bring a lot of rain at certain times of the year, and none at other times. They occur near the equator.

Monsoons bring heavy rain when the Sun is overhead. The Sun heats the land intensely at this time, and warmed air rises. Moist air from over the sea rushes in to replace it – this rushing air forms the monsoon winds. Cumulonimbus clouds form in the rising air, bringing heavy rain. Occasionally the monsoon rains do not come, which causes drought.

In winter, the Sun is no longer overhead and the land cools. Dry winds blow from the land out to sea, and the land becomes very dry. In India, the land becomes parched and cracked during winter. People wait anxiously for the summer rains to come. When they do, they are very happy.

Weather Report

Monsoon rains bring happiness but also some anxiety, because too much rain causes floods.

Heavy monsoonal rains caused chaos in Amritsar, India.

Farming conditions in Australia are often severely affected by drought. Farmers have to buy feed so their livestock can survive.

Droughts

When an area has a lot less rainfall than usual, for a long period of time such as months or years, we say there is a drought. During a drought:

- the soil dries out
- water supplies such as rivers, lakes, waterholes and creeks dry up.
- it is difficult for people to grow crops and find feed for animals.

Some droughts last for many years.

Drought can lead to the spreading of deserts, which causes **erosion** and brings dust storms. It also brings wildfires to dry **woodlands** and grasslands.

In poor countries, drought can leave many people with not enough food to eat. This brings illnesses and deaths from starvation. In countries such as Australia, New Zealand and the United States, drought has caused hardship for many farmers.

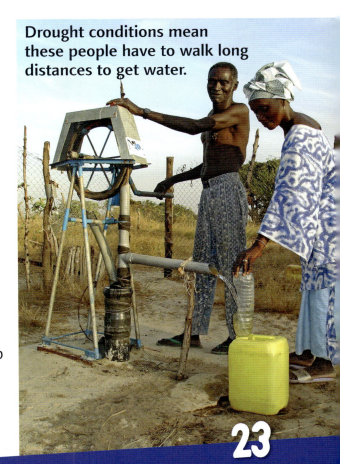

Drought conditions mean these people have to walk long distances to get water.

Floods and landslides

Too much water causes floods, landslides and mudslides. These damage or destroy people's homes and land, towns and villages. Floods wash away or damage buildings, while landslides and mudslides can bury them.

Floods

Floods occur when rivers overflow, when there is sudden heavy rain and when huge waves from storm surges cover the coast. Unfortunately, all of these things can happen at the same time.

Rivers may flood because there has been a lot of rain, or because of snow melting in the mountains. Sudden heavy rain usually comes from slow-moving thunderstorms that drop huge amounts of rain over a small area in a short time, causing flash flooding.

During tropical storms such as hurricanes and cyclones, the storm surge and huge waves, together with very heavy rain, bring floods to coastlines. The sea can break through **dikes** and **levees** during storms.

Weather Report

Some rivers flood regularly. The area they flood is called a 'flood plain'.

Bangladesh has had devastating floods that have killed many people and made many more homeless.

Landslides

A landslide can take place when heavy rain has weakened the ground on the side of a hill or mountain. Rocks, soil and plants break free and slide down the hill. Homes on the side of the hill slide down with the landslide, and homes at the bottom can get covered with rocks and dirt. People who live on the sides of steep valleys are at most risk from landslides.

A mudslide is similar to a landslide but it is wetter and muddier. In a mudslide, a muddy mixture of rock and soil can flow quite a long way, and may cover land, homes and villages.

This mudslide destroyed the town of Guinsahugon, on the island of Leyte in the Philippines in 2006.

Ice and snow

Winter blizzards are common in northern parts of the United States.

During winter, blizzards and ice storms occur over large areas of Europe and North America.

Blizzards

Blizzards are snowstorms with strong winds, heavy snowfalls and temperatures below zero degrees Celsius. It is dangerous to be in a blizzard, as it brings deep snow, it is very difficult to see far, and the wind is so cold it can be deadly. Blizzards interrupt daily life because they stop transport, and they overload the power supply because people need to turn up their heating.

Weather Report

The coldest places on Earth are the north and south **polar** areas and the very high mountaintops. The temperature in these places is usually below freezing point all year round.

It can be dangerous to be out in a blizzard like this one in Helsinki, Finland.

Ice storms

An ice storm happens when rain freezes as it hits the ground. It occurs when rain falls from clouds in air that is only a little warmer than **freezing point** through air just above the ground which is below freezing point. This causes the rain to freeze and coats the ground and other surfaces with a layer of ice. Ice storms make roads and paths slippery and dangerous.

Ice pellets

Ice pellets are small balls of ice made from raindrops that freeze as they fall through freezing air near the ground. Falls of ice pellets are called 'sleet' in North America. In other parts of the world, sleet is the name for falling wet snow.

Ice storm damage affected four central states in the United States, in December 2007.

Heatwaves and wildfires

Many places on Earth have hot weather during summer. People say there is a heatwave when the weather becomes much hotter than usual, over a period of a few days or weeks. Humidity is often higher during a heatwave.

Heatwaves cause many health problems for people, especially very old, very young, or sick people. They can suffer from heat exhaustion, **heat stroke**, dehydration, heat rashes and swellings. Many people have died during heatwaves.

Weather Report

Places on or near Earth's equator have very hot climates. In some of these areas, such as in hot deserts, daytime temperatures can often reach 50 degrees Celsius.

Dangerous heatwaves

The United States had a serious heatwave in July 2006. Temperatures in some parts of South Dakota were higher than 46 degrees Celsius and Los Angeles, California reached 49 degrees Celsius.

In 2006, there was also a serious heatwave in Europe. Temperatures rose to 40 degrees Celsius in Paris. Germany had temperatures of 35 degrees Celsius, while the United Kingdom recorded 37 degrees Celsius.

High temperatures can cause rail lines to buckle, making them unsafe.

Wildfires

Often heatwaves bring wildfires, especially if the vegetation has dried out from a drought, and there is strong wind.

Fires spread easily in areas that have eucalyptus trees. This is because eucalyptus oil is very **flammable**. These trees are common in the Australian bush, which is one reason why wildfires are common in the Australian summer.

Wildfires are often started by lightning. They are also started by people. People may start fires deliberately, or they may accidentally leave camp fires burning. Unfortunately, sometimes wildfires have been started by officials when burn-offs have accidentally got out of control.

Flames sometimes rush upwards so fast they form a whirl, like a tornado. This is called a 'fire whirl' or 'fire tornado'. A fire whirl can make a wildfire even more dangerous.

Wildfires are common in the Australian summer.

Weather wonders

Tropical storms have a spiral shape. They are between 400 and 800 kilometres in diameter. Winds can reach 200 kilometres per hour or more.

The longest lightning bolt ever recorded was 190 kilometres long.

The most violent tornadoes have wind speeds of more than 480 kilometres per hour. They are more than 1.6 kilometres across, and stay on the ground for more than 100 kilometres.

A hurricane, cyclone or typhoon has sustained wind speeds of at least 119 kilometres per hour. The fastest sustained wind speeds are 314 kilometres per hour.

The coldest air temperature ever recorded was minus 89.6 degrees Celsius at Vostok Station, in Antarctica, in 1983.

The warmest air temperature ever recorded was 58 degrees Celsius, in Libya, in 1922.

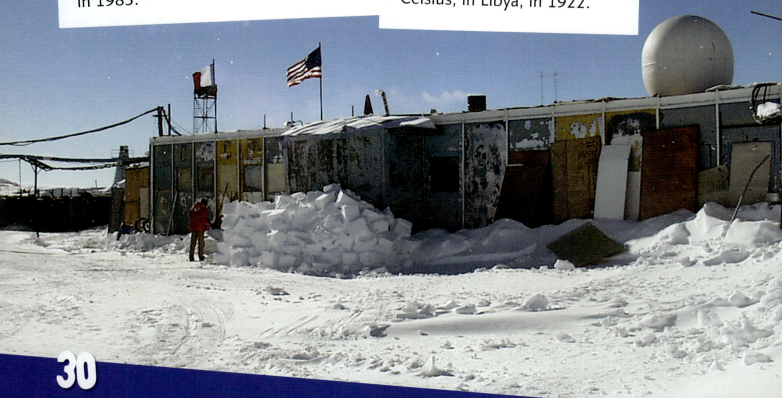

Glossary

bolts lightning sparks

Celsius a scale of temperature measurement

charges build ups of electricity

cold front when a colder air mass approaches a warmer air mass. The colder air, being more dense, cuts a wedge under the less dense warmer air, lifting it and finally overtaking it. Cold fronts move rapidly.

condenses changes from a gas to a liquid

crystals pieces of pure substance

deserts very dry areas that receive very little rainfall

dikes walls beside water bodies to keep water from flooding the land

droughts periods of time when there is a much less rainfall than usual

equator imaginary line around the middle of Earth that divides the Northern and Southern Hemispheres

erosion when soil is carried away by wind or water

evaporate change from a liquid to a gas

flammable catches fire easily

freezing point zero degrees Celsius; the temperature at which water freezes

glaciers huge rivers of ice made of hardened snow

heatstroke illness caused by being too hot, causing breathing difficulties and dizziness

humid moist air

levees walls beside water bodies to keep water from flooding land

polar parts of Earth at the top and bottom of the globe

radar equipment that sends out signals to detect how far away something is

satellite spacecraft that circles Earth

sirens loudspeakers that make a loud wailing sound

tropical in the area on or near Earth's equator

troposphere lowest layer of the atmosphere that rises to about 10 kilometres above Earth's surface

waterspout tornado that occurs over water, which it sucks up

water vapour water particles in the air

woodlands area with trees that are not very close together

Index

A
Antarctica   6, 30

B
blizzards   26

C
climate   4, 5, 28
cloud   6, 7, 11, 14, 17, 20
cold front   7
cumulonimbus   6, 7, 17, 22
cyclones   16, 17, 24, 30

D
desert   5, 20, 23, 28
downdraft   7, 8
drought   5, 20, 22, 23, 28
dust storm   20, 23

F
fire tornado   29
floods   5, 16, 19, 22, 24

H
hail   6, 8
hailstones   8, 9, 30
heatwave   5, 28, 29
humidity   28
hurricanes   16, 17, 24, 30

I
ice   5, 7, 8, 9, 26, 27
ice pellet   9, 27
ice storm   26, 27

L
landslides   24, 25
lightning   6, 7, 10, 11, 14, 16, 17, 29, 30

M
monsoons   22
mudslides   24, 25

R
radar   14
rain   6, 8, 9, 16, 17, 18, 19, 22, 24, 25, 27
raindrops   8, 27
rivers   23, 24

S
sandstorm   20
satellite   19
showers   8
sleet   27
snow   4, 5, 24, 26, 27
storm surge   18, 19, 24
Sun   22

T
thunder   6, 10, 16, 17
thunderclouds   6, 7, 8, 9, 11, 12, 13, 14, 15, 17, 18, 21
thunderstorms   6, 7, 9, 10, 12, 16, 18, 20, 24
tornado spotters   14
tornado warnings   14
tornado watchers   14
tornadoes   12, 13, 14, 15, 21, 30
tropical storms   16, 17, 18, 19, 24, 30
tropics   16
troposphere   6
typhoons   16, 17, 30

U
updrafts   7, 8

W
waterspouts   15
waves   16, 18, 21, 24
whirlwinds   20, 21
wildfires   23, 28, 29
winds   6, 7, 8, 12, 16, 17, 18, 19, 20, 21, 22, 26